TROKOSI

Marty D. Fish

"The wind; it runs away and no one captures it; no one can master it; it is no one's slave. It belongs to no one... be the wind."

Contents

TROKOSI

Preface

My name *was* Afi Nunana, of the Ewe people, from the Republic of Togo. I tell you my name *was*, because I am no longer that small girl, who became a Trokosi at the age of eight. I am no longer called by that name; you will see. If you wonder what a *Trokosi* is, I will tell you. A Trokosi is a slave of the gods. I was such a slave. This is my story.

TROKOSI

Chapter 1

Sex Slave

Not long ago, in my remote jungle village in Africa, I was forced to become a sex slave to a powerful Vodun priest, Kuuku Mawa-Lisu, in a shrine temple. I was his Trokosi for many years. I became a slave because my sister before me was a slave and she died at the temple. It was my duty to replace her, to pay for my father's sin. Kuuku beat her to death for not bowing before him; at least that is what I was told. Kuuku was my master; he would beat me too if I did not tell him that he was my god; I did not disobey. He told me that I was blessed, because I was "Nyui," which means beautiful, and he lay with me. It made me the wife of a god. I was not the only one. There were many of us. I have lived and suffered much because of his blessings.

TROKOSI

Chapter 2

The Curse of the Gods

Before I was born, my father, a cassava farmer, believed he had been cursed by the gods. For several years, many bad things happened to him. In the first season of the curse, his crops were destroyed. He said this was the curse of Agê. The following year, fire fell from the sky onto the straw roof of our hut; it burned to the ground. Father said this was the curse of Xêvioso. The next year, my father was cursed with the disease AIDS. He said he had not had relations with anyone other than my mother, but that it was the last curse of the god Sakpata, before he would die. My mother, crying on her knees, pleaded with father to go to the Vodun priest to have the curse removed. Fearing for his life, he did.

Kuuku Mawa-Lisu, the priest, was considered a Dzon'ku, a great sorcerer in our village; this is unusual among our people. Sorcerers and priests are rarely one and the same. Kuuku was feared by all and very powerful. It was known among all that if he was angry, he could gaze upon you with the eye of Dangbe and you would die that night. Those he had cursed publicly disappeared in the night, never to been seen again. The villagers said that his curses caused the gods to come down and drag away the evil-doers to a pit of torment and punishment. When I was a small girl, I remember my father telling me of such a story.

"Once a year," my father said, "all the village men present great sacrifices unto Kuuku, to appease the gods for the sins of their families. It happens after the time of harvest. Many moons ago, there was an elder who sold plantains in the marketplace. He was well-respected in our village. I do not know why, but one day he refused to give the sacrifice unto the gods. The priests surrounded his hut with torches of fire and demanded that he make his sacrifice before the sun arose, or they would burn him and his family alive in the hut. The elder agreed to make the sacrifice. When the dawn came, Kuuku found a cart of plantains from the elder at the temple door. He reached into the cart to take one, but the plantains were rotten and they rested on a pile

of monkey dung. It was the greatest insult to
the gods that one could make. The elder had
defied the gods. Kuuku's scream could be
heard from all over the village. In a rage,
Kuuku bursts into flames; great wings split out
of his back. His eyes turned red as the
bloodstone. He flew as a fire god to the elder's
hut. Kuuku clapped his hands together and
the whole earth shook. The earth tore apart;
fire spit out of the pit and swallowed the
elder's hut and everyone in his family. Devil
dogs from the pit dragged the elder and his
family alive into the flames. Kuuku clapped
his hands together once more and the earth
closed upon them. They were never to be seen
again. To this day, they burn alive in the pit of
the devil dogs. This is what happens to those
who defy the gods and who refuse to sacrifice
unto Kuuku." Such stories made my father
live in great fear of Kuuku and the gods.

My father pled with the god Kuuku to meet
with him and he agreed. My father fell on his
face before Kuuku in the temple and he told
him of his curse. Kuuku walked around my
father and knelt down to draw magical Vodun
symbols in the dust. Kuuku told him that he

knew the source of the three curses. He said that the gods were not pleased, because he had neglected his sacrifice to the temple. Kuuku said that my father was to die and his family to die as well.

In the temple, my father begged Kuuku to have mercy and plead to the gods for him. Kuuku said that he would relent and be merciful, beseeching the gods, if my father was willing to make great sacrifice for his sins. My father cried to him that he would do whatever the gods required. Kuuku demanded that my father make atonement by giving three daughters, my older sisters, to him to become his priestesses. The priestesses are what our people call Trokosi.

My father had many children before me. He agreed to this great sacrifice. Father was told to cut off his hair and give it to Kuuku, along with a goat and three chickens. The priest performed a public ceremonial ritual to remove the curses from my family. He sacrificed the goat and chickens to the gods, pouring the blood out upon the hair, before all the people. The goat was sacrificed to appease the great father god Mawu; the chickens were sacrificed to appease the gods Agê, Xêvioso, and Sakpata. Kuuku buried my father's hair with the blood in three different places around the shrine temple. This meant that my father's sins were covered by the sacrifice and buried before the gods at the temple, so that they would remember them no more.

The servants of the priests played the ceremonial drums and Kuuku fell into a trance and danced among the priestesses to call upon the gods for their blessing. He blew a sacred white powder of blessing over my family and declared to the entire village that there was no more curse. My father had been saved; that is what Kuuku told him; everyone believed.

The next season, I was born. My mother told me that I was a sign that my family had become blessed by the gods once again; I was a gift from the gods. That is why they named me Nunana; which means *gift*. I was very loved and well-treated.

Before I knew my three elder sisters, they became Trokosi and were never to be seen by our family again. I did not even know of this, until I was eight years old. That is when the priest came to my father's hut. He told my father that my eldest sister had displeased the gods and had died, because she would not bow before him. Kuuku told him that if I did not replace her, the curses would return tenfold and my father would die that night. He, fearing greatly, gave me unto the priest.

I was afraid and ran to my mother and begged her to save me. I cried, "Do not let him take me, mother." She was afraid, too, but knew there was no other way. She held me and whispered into my ear, "The wind; it runs away and no one captures it; no one can master it; it is no one's slave. It belongs to no one. The day will come, when the time is right, that you must be the wind." She turned to the priest, bowed down low before him and said, "Mawuga Kuuku, the great and powerful, if you take my daughter, please grant this one request." This was unusual, because it is not customary to call the priest Mawuga, which means "Great God," and women dared not speak to him. But, it pleased him and he answered her, "What is it?" She begged, "Afi is the first of our family to go to school. Please allow her to continue her studies that she may better serve you. I fear that my eldest failed you because she was not educated enough to understand your greatness."

The priest looked down at her and replied, "Very well. I will grant your wish, so that Afi may not fail me as your other daughter did." She cried, "Thank you, Mawuga Kuuku. As I will never see her again, before you take Afi, may I hold her one last time in my arms?" He nodded. She pulled me close to her and I cried. She said, "Zi, dodoe," which means, "Be silent." I quieted down and mother whispered, "Aya … nogbe aya tso de ame nu Mawu … aya," which means, "One day you will rise up like the wind and revolt against even the gods… you will be the wind." Then, like the wind, I was taken away.

TROKOSI

Chapter 3

Sisters of the Dream

I had become the slave of the gods. At the shrine temple, I met my two elder sisters; I was anxious to do so, but they did not know me; they did not even know I was their sister. They did not care that we were related at all. Their eyes looked like they were empty souls, what we call in our village the Zombi, or walking dead. But they were not the only ones. Most of the elder Trokosi had the same look of death in their eyes.

It was secretly said among the Trokosi that if you served the priest long enough and could not please him, you would become soulless. It was the curse of the serpent god, Dangbe. That is where the word Zombi comes from. It is said that Kuuku could turn people into the Zombi by the power of the serpent god. There is a legend among my village that many years ago, an elder priestess of the temple came to Kuuku and demanded her release to go into the world. He agreed, but when she turned to walk away, he called upon Dangbe.

Immediately, as she stepped out of the temple, she became the Zombi. Some of the village people say they have seen her corpse at night walking among the dead spirits in the darkest parts of the jungle. This is why the Trokosi fear Kuuku and dare not displease him.

After a few seasons at the temple, I heard that my father passed away; he died of AIDS. But, I do not know what happened to my mother or other siblings. I was told they were taken by the gods because of his great sin. Only I was spared, because I was under the protection of the god Kuuku. Although my father died and the gods did not heal him as Kuuku promised, I was not released from the temple service. This is because once a child becomes the property of the priest, she belongs to him forever.

I lived as a slave of Kuuku for many years, serving him completely, fearing for my life. I dared not displease him, because I knew he had the power of life and death. Frequently, he would beat one of the other slaves with his staff, because they were foolish. I was beaten too, on occasion, but lightly and less often than most. Unlike some, I was only beaten when I deserved it. The other Trokosi told me it was because I was his blessed one and he wanted to keep me unmarked for the sowing of his great seed.

Kuuku did allow me to attend *suku,* or school, as he promised; it was my only escape. School was my salvation, but I had to act ignorant, because education was looked down upon among the Trokosi and priests. Many were jealous, because I was the only Trokosi who was allowed to attend school. Some priests were angry with Kuuku, because he allowed me to have books and go to school. They felt it threatened their own power and authority over their slaves, but they did not dare confront him; Kuuku was feared by all. I worked harder than all the other Trokosi to please Kuuku. I knew I had to prove to him that I was more faithful, because I went to school. I hoped that by doing so, he might allow some of the other Trokosi to attend too, but he never did. He only allowed me to, because he knew I would not betray him.

At the shrine, I heard the tales of how my elder sister suffered and died by his hand; I did everything to gain his complete trust. I was the example to all the Trokosi in how to worship Kuuku and adore him. Like my mother, I called him Mawuga Kuuku. He liked this very much.

Outside of school, I spent my time serving in the temple cooking, cleaning, and fetching water for Kuuku. He would not let me do the farming or caring for the livestock like the other girls. They were afraid of me, because I had Kuuku's eye. I did not treat them badly, though. I tried to be kind to all of them, because I knew they were suffering silently, like me. Some of them were there for the same reasons I was, but others were born in the temple as the offspring of the slaves. They were called the Trokosiviwo. This means they were born slaves and would be so all their lives, because they were the property of the priest. When Kuuku died, they would become the property of the next priest and so on. This is the tradition.

One night, when I was twelve, as I always did, I slept in the slave chamber with some of the girls and sang songs to them. These were songs that my mother had taught to me. One of the girls was only four years old and had just come to us; her name was Sosi. She was crying and afraid. My singing helped Sosi to sleep. After she fell asleep, another Trokosi named Akosua asked me, "Afi, how is it that you are so strong? Why do you show no fear?" I told her, "Akosua, I am always afraid. I am no different than you. But, I do have one secret." She said, "Tell me, what is that secret?" I explained, "When Kuuku came to take me away, I was scared for my life. My mother told me this secret. She said, 'The wind; it runs away and no one captures it; no one can master it; it is no one's slave. It belongs to no one. The day will come, when the time is right that you must be the wind.' Akosua, I have this hope. This is why I can be afraid, but can be strong; this is why I show no fear. I am patient and serve Kuuku, but one day, I will be the wind. I will not be here forever. You see, one day I will fly as the wind and no one will capture me. The day will come, but the time must be right and on that day, I will be no one's slave; no one will master me."

Akosua became excited and told me, "Afi, I want that hope. I want to become the wind

too. Do you think this is possible?" I told her
to be silent, "... It is not only possible, it will
happen; I know it." The girls became excited
and I told them to quiet down again. What
they were learning was new to them and I
realized at that moment that this hope that I
saw in their eyes was dangerous. It caused
them to realize something new: the truth. In
our world, realization of such truth is
dangerous for a slave. It is what causes
Trokosi to become free in their hearts, but to
become beaten and abused in their bodies.
Truth and knowledge to a slave is death.

Their eyes had changed from darkness of
despair to a glint of hope. They would never
be the same. I told them to hush and go to
sleep. But from that moment on, I was not
alone in my dream. Akosua, Sosi, and I
became sisters of the dream and we had a hope
that none of the other Trokosi had, or
understood. We would become the winds of
Africa and fly away from that place one day. It
was our hope.

Chapter 4

Suku Nufiala

My schooling was done mostly outside, under an open thatched hut. It was small, but I was always excited to learn. Our teacher was from our village, but had travelled to other places beyond the jungle. He was respected by all and considered to be a wise and knowledgeable man. His name was Papa Wati, but we called him Nufiala, which means teacher. He was a great and kind man. Nufiala was not like any man I had ever known. He was not afraid of anyone or anything. He did not even seem to fear the gods. I wanted to learn at his feet always, but after school I had to return to the temple.

Being the only Trokosi at school was not easy. I was feared by all the other children, because they considered me the priestess of the great Kuuku. They avoided me because they thought I had magical powers. But, this confused me, because I had no powers at all. How could I be feared and thought to have magic when it was not true? I never told them

27

I had the Vodun powers, but they believed it. I began to wonder about the power of belief. Among the children, I could have made them fear me even more if I chose to, but I did not.

Most of the school children in my village go to school to learn how to tend livestock, or to become farmers, or fishermen. In the jungle, there is much rain and it is a good place to grow crops. Farming plantain, cassava, and rice is common in my village. Those who learn to farm or tend livestock must also learn the ways of the jungle, so they may be safe from the wild animals and plants. This is also necessary to protect the livestock. In the jungle, the plants are more dangerous than the animals. Many young children have suffered death by eating poisonous berries or by touching cursed plants. In school, Nufiala spent much time teaching us about the dangerous plants and animals. He taught us that although some plants were deadly to eat, other plants could ward off their death attack, so that one could eat the deadly plant, but eat the good plant and live. School taught us many great and wonderful things like this.

There was a school boy named Kofi, who studied to be a farmer and he knew much about these jungle plants; more than anyone in the village. Nufiala asked Kofi to stand up and show some of his plants to the class. Kofi was much larger and older than me. As he got up with his basket of plants, he tripped and fell upon me, as I was sitting on the ground. I was not hurt, but he was scared and fell before me, begging me to forgive him. I did not know what to do. I was not angry or hurt. I said, "I forgive you." He crawled away picking up his basket as though he were afraid; the children also looked at me in great fear. I looked up at Nufiala, confused, and he smiled at me. When school was over, Nufiala asked me to meet with him, so I did.

After the children left, Nufiala said to me, "Afi, why do you think Kofi was afraid of you?" I replied, "I do not know." He continued, "He is a very large boy, the largest in our village; what did he think you could do to him?" Again, I said, "I do not know. Can you tell me?" Nufiala explained, "It is because he *believes* you are something you are not; all the children do. Let me ask you, Afi, if he had hurt you, could you have called the Vodun gods to kill or curse him?" I said, "No, I have no powers; I am only a Trokosi. Mawuga Kuuku could do this if he wanted to, but not me. I would not hurt anyone."

"Afi, I know that you would not. You are a good girl and a good student. But, what if you were not? If you had wanted to, you could have stood up before Kofi and he might have worshipped you, just like the villagers worship Kuuku. Did you realize that?" I said, "No, I did not, but why would he worship me?" Nufiala explained, "It is because of one thing, *belief*." I said, "Belief?" "Yes, belief is a very powerful thing. I will show you. Fetch me a large stone."

I found a stone on the ground and handed it to him. He said, "Do you believe that this stone has Vodun powers?" I said, "No." He said, "Do you believe it is a sacred charm and can ward off spirits and prevent curses?" I said, "No, Nufiala, it is only a stone." "Afi, I am going to teach you a new lesson, but it is only for you. You must promise not to tell anyone about this lesson; do you promise?" I was excited to learn and I said, "Yes, what is it?" He held up the stone and said, "You will see. Always remember what you first believed about this stone. Tomorrow, the lesson begins." Then I went back to the temple.

TROKOSI

Chapter 5

The Lesson of the Stone

The evening after I spoke to Nufiala, I wondered what my lesson would be. As I worked, I could not stop thinking about the stone. What could he teach me with a stone? It was not a useful stone; it was just a stone.

Again, I sang to Sosi and Akosua until they fell asleep; it had become a tradition. I lay next to Sosi and watched her sleep; she was so peaceful and small. She did not yet understand how powerful, great, and fearful Kuuku was. I wish I could have been like her. She was free like the wind. Yet, I knew that she would grow up like us, learning how to fear Kuuku and the gods.

I thought about fear, the gods, and the boy Kofi. I wondered why Kofi was afraid of me. I had not done anything to cause him fear. I was not a large girl; I was a slave girl. I wondered if the way he felt about me was the way we felt about Kuuku. I put it away from my mind. It was not possible. I was just a girl; Kuuku was a god.

The next day, I went to school very anxious. When I arrived, I saw the stone on top of a sacred Vodun stool, in the front, and in the middle of class. Behind it was a small bowl of sacred oil, burning. I was confused when I saw it. I looked at Nufiala and he smiled and told me to sit down; I obeyed.

As class began, I wondered what the stone was doing sitting on the sacred stool. I noticed that the children also wondered. They all began to talk among themselves. Nufiala told the students to be silent; they did, but we were anxious to know. For the whole class day, Nufiala taught us as usual, but he did not say anything about the stone. He did not look at it or talk about it. After class was over, I approached him and said, "Nufiala, I am ready to begin my lesson of the stone." He said, "Your lesson has begun; you are dismissed." I was confused; I obeyed and left to go to the temple.

The next day, I went to school and the same thing happened. The children were growing more curious about the stone. I was, too. As the class continued, we could not focus on what Nufiala was teaching. He had to stop class and tell one child to stop staring at the stone. But we all could not. By the end of the day, one student became brave and asked Nufiala what the stone was there for. Nufiala replied, "I cannot tell you. It is a secret. But I will tell you that the stone was given to me by a servant of the great Kuuku." I did not understand at all; that servant was me. But, they did not realize that. They looked at it in fear, which caused me to become more confused and also afraid. But why? I did not know. I did not understand what was going on; even I was becoming anxious about the stone. But it was nothing but a stone.

As the days went on, the children grew more fearful. They could not do their work because of the stone. Some of the children stopped coming to class. I heard two children talking about the stone. One said it was cursed; the other said it was the eye of Dangbe, watching us. He said that the gods were using it to see if we were being good or bad; that is why Kuuku sent it to the class to watch us. I could not understand what I was hearing. These children were foolish, but I was not to say a word.

35

After class, I went to Nufiala. I said, "Do you know what the children are saying about this stone?" He replied, "Yes, Afi, I am aware, but what do you think about the stone?" I said, "I do not know. It is just a stone. I picked it up from the ground." He said, "Why do you not know, then?" I responded, "It is because of how the children talk. They are afraid of it." He said, "Why, Afi? Why are they afraid of it?" I said, "I do not know." He said, "Afi, this is just the beginning of your lesson. But, you must remember what you first believed about the stone. You are dismissed."

The next day, in class, one child was sitting next to the stone as though he were in a trance staring at it; he began screaming and ran away crying. It caused us all to be frightened. Nufiala told us all to be silent, but the children could not be. He tried to teach, but no one was listening. He said that we were dismissed. One girl began crying as she left and said that we should not be in the presence of the god's eye. I watched them all leave. I sat there watching it all happen, not understanding why everyone was so afraid. Nufiala looked at me and said, "Afi, what have you learned so far in your lesson of the stone?" I looked back at him and said, "I am very confused. I do not know." He said, "What do you see here on this stool? Is it just a stone?" I replied, "I thought it was just a stone. Am I wrong?" He said, "Do not forget what you first believed. You are dismissed."

The next day, fewer children showed up to school. Then, something unusual happened. Several village men came to the school and told Nufiala that he must remove the sacred stone from the school grounds or their children could not attend. They told him that curses were coming down from the gods upon their village, because the stone was not in its holy place. Nufiala told them that it was given to him by a servant of the great Kuuku and it would remain there until the gods came to take it away. They were angered and told him that the school was cursed, but they left. They were afraid. After that, all the children ran away from the school. The whole village was growing afraid of the stone.

What I was watching and learning was strange. How could a common stone cause men to act so afraid and foolish? That night, after I had fallen asleep with the other Trokosi, I heard loud shouts and screams outside the shrine temple. We awoke, startled. I went outside the chamber to see what was happening. There, in front of the temple was a large group of village men, with torches, calling out to Kuuku. When he awoke, he went outside to confront them, "What is it that you want?" They fell down on the ground before him in worship; one cried, "Great Kuuku, we beg you to save us from the eye of Dangbe." He responded, "And what is this that you are talking about?" He said, "One of your servants brought the sacred stone to the school and it has cursed the whole village. God, we beg of you to return it to the holy temple, so that we may be blessed once again." Kuuku looked out among the people. Everyone became silent. He did not say a word.

After a long while, he spoke. Kuuku said, "You will take me to this stone and I will remove the curse, but you must first make sacrifices to the temple, to appease the gods." The village men all cried out to him, "We will do what you wish." He told them, "Every man of every household in the village must bring me one child, goat, or great offering tomorrow morning after the sun rises. If the offerings please the gods, I will remove the curse by the setting of the sun. If not, each of your families will suffer the curse of the eye of Dangbe." Then he returned to the temple.

I watched Kuuku tell the village that he would remove the curse, but there was no curse to remove. I had picked up a stone from the ground and it had become the eye of a god. How could this be? It caused me great concern. Could the stone have become the eye of a god from the time I picked it up? Or, could it be that the people were crazy? Could Kuuku have believed it himself? I could not bring myself to think that he could be lying, because he was a god and gods cannot lie. We did not have school the next day, but my lesson continued, even though I did not realize that I was being taught.

At sunrise, all the people of the village were at the front of the temple, bringing great sacrifices to Kuuku, to appease the gods. Some brought baskets of plantains, carts of rice, goats, chickens, goods, and even children to give unto Kuuku. It took many hours to collect all the offerings. At noon, Kuuku announced unto the village that the gods were pleased by the sacrifices and that he would perform a ceremony that night to remove the curse of the stone.

Kuuku had all the Trokosi and priests prepare for the ritual. At sundown, the priests sat down and we, the priestesses, danced around them while the drums played. This was to bring the attention of the gods upon our village. Then, Kuuku went into a deep trance; he led a procession of drums and dance from the temple to the school, where the stone rested upon the stool. He blew sacred powder around the school grounds and around the stool. His priests lifted the stone from off the stool with sacred leaves and placed the stone into a sacred basket. He sacrificed a goat in front of the school and poured its blood on the ground around it. He declared that the curse had been removed. The priests carried the basket back to the temple and put the stone into the shrine. It was announced unto all that the stone was part of the sacred shrine and would be under the protection of the gods.

The people shouted and celebrated the entire night, because the gods had blessed them once again. But I did not celebrate. I was confused as I tried to learn the lesson of the stone. It was a greater lesson than I could understand or bring myself to believe.

The next day, I went to the school and many of the children had returned. It was as if nothing had happened. Everything was back to normal, though the stool was no longer there. Nufiala taught us as though everything was as it were before the lesson of the stone. But the stone that I picked up from the ground was now a sacred eye of the gods and was guarded by the priests in the shrine. How could that be?

After class, I went to Nufiala and begged, "Please explain to me what I saw in the lesson of the stone." He said, "Afi, what do you think you saw?" I said, "I picked up a stone and it became the eye of Dangbe. The stone I picked up from the ground is now in the temple shrine. How could that be?" He said, "What did you first believe?" I said, "I first believed that it was only a stone." He responded, "And you are correct. It *is* only a stone. I put it on a sacred stool and I did not lie to anyone about it. I only told them that it was given to me by a servant of Kuuku. Is that not true?" I said, "Yes." He said, "What you saw happen was what the children *chose* to believe. All the people chose to believe that the stone was greater than it truly was." I said, "But why?" He replied, "That is a good question. Now what you must discover is why people *believe*. Now remember, Afi, before we started your lesson, Kofi fell upon you and was afraid of you. Do you remember why?" I responded, "You said it was because he *believed* I was something that I am not." He said, "That is correct. That is the same reason that the people feared the stone. It is because they believed it was something that it is not. Only you and I know the truth about the stone. Now you must learn the lesson of the gods. But, that is a lesson you must learn on your own. I will not teach you that lesson. I have already taught you enough." Then, he dismissed me and sent me away to consider my new lesson.

Chapter 6

The Lesson of the Gods

That night, I lay next to Akosua and Sosi, but I could not sleep. I whispered, "Akosua, are you asleep?" She awoke, "What is it, Afi?" I said, "I did not want to wake you; I cannot sleep." She said, "What is bothering you?" I replied, "It is the stone." She said, "The stone? Yes, I know; everyone is talking about it; it is very powerful... the eye of Dangbe..." I responded, "Akosua, how do you know that?" She said, "It is because of the great curse it brought upon our people, but is now gone. Kuuku saved us from its stare of death."

I did not know how to respond. I lay there silently for a while. I whispered, "Akosua, can you keep a secret?" She said, "Yes, what is it?" I sat up and leaned over her and said, "You must promise by death of the gods not to tell a soul... ever!" She looked at me frightened, but said, "Yes... I promise you." I continued, "What if I told you that the stone was not from the gods... but, from me?" She looked surprised, "Afi, be silent! You will bring down the curse of Dangbe upon us!" I said, "No, Akosua, it is true! I picked up the stone from the ground and gave it to Nufiala at school. The next day, he placed it on the sacred stool. Every day, the children made up stories about it until everyone believed it was the eye of Dangbe." She said, "That is not possible. It was given to Nufiala by the servant of Kuuku himself!" I said, "Yes, that servant is me. Nufiala took the stone from me to teach me a lesson." She looked at me confused and said, "Why would he do that? If it was not the eye of Dangbe, Kuuku would have known. He would not have had to perform the great ritual to deliver the whole village from the curse."

I lay back down next to her and we both lay silent for a moment. I spoke, "This is why I cannot sleep. The stone is only a stone, but it is now in the sacred shrine. Everyone believes it is the eye of Dangbe. Nufiala told me that the lesson of the stone is over and that I must learn a new lesson, the lesson of the gods. But he will not tell me what that lesson is. I do not understand." Akosua whispered back, "If that stone was not the eye of Dangbe, then Kuuku must have known. A god would have known that. How could he be god, if he did not know?" We were silent again.

I looked up at the straw roof and thought about the possibility of Kuuku not being a god. It was an impossibility to conceive, but I could now see how he might not be. I remembered what my mother told me when I was a young girl; she said that I would one day rise up like the wind and revolt against even the gods. I never understood that. Maybe she knew the lesson of the gods. Why else would she tell me that I would one day revolt against the gods? I whispered to Akosua, who now could not sleep either, "I just want to be the wind and fly away from here." She said, "Afi, one day, we will... both of us. We will fly together like the wind, far away from this place and we will be free." I turned my head and smiled at her. She was like my sister; we held hands as sisters do. In the late hours, Akosua finally fell asleep. I did not.

I thought about everything I had learned from Nufiala. I thought about my eldest sister, who I never met, but wondered if it could have been the same lesson that caused her to defy Kuuku. She had refused to bow down before him. Why would she do that? The only reason I could imagine that anyone would not bow down to a god, is if he was not really a god at all. Could it be that she realized that he was not really god, but a man? I tried to reject the thought, since it was blasphemy; but I could not. My school teacher had taught me to ask questions and to think, but Trokosi were not allowed to think. I could not help it; I thought too much.

Just what if Kuuku was not really god? This could not be, but if my sister thought it were true, it could have caused her to defy him. And, if she did, it could have caused him to fear her and what she would make the other slaves realize about him. Maybe this is why she was murdered by him. I did not hate him, though. My mother taught me that hate was a cursed spirit serpent. She said that if you go to sleep with hate in your soul, a spirit serpent will come in the night with fiery red eyes; he would slither down your throat and wrap himself around your heart and choke it within your chest, a little each day, until you die. She said hate always kills; I believed it. I chose not to hate, but to become the wind and fly away

from Kuuku one day. But it was not time. I
must wait.

TROKOSI

Chapter 7

Trokosi of Sacrifice

In the shrine temple, it was common to find serpents at night. The serpents came from the jungle to eat mice, rats, chickens, and small goats. The priests did not mind, as these were considered minor sacrifices to appease the gods. Kuuku taught us that every now and then, Dangbe would come down as the great serpent and he would take a sacrifice from among the Trokosi. This was a great sacrifice and it was an honor to be the chosen Trokosi of sacrifice. He said Dangbe only took pure, young virgins and when he did, it meant that all the Trokosi were cleansed of their sins until he returned.

Such tales caused us to live in great fear and wonder of the gods. But, I thought often of my mother's words about how she foretold that I would one day rise up and revolt against the gods. How could that be? No one dared defy the gods, but how is it that my mother believed this could be so? Maybe her rebellion was the sin of my family, why my father died,

and why she was swept away by the gods. I
could not believe that, though. Mother was a
good woman. She was kind and took great
care of us children. This was a mystery that I
hid in my soul. It was not one that I could
even ask the gods an answer for, without
bringing down their wrath upon me.

Another season passed and I thought upon
these things. I learned from Nufiala, a little
more every day. Akosua and I talked together
late many nights, quietly learning the lesson of
the gods, until one night, the lesson was
revealed.

Except for the scampering of mice on the
thatched roof, it was silent in the temple; all the
Trokosi were asleep. Even I was in deep sleep
that night, until I heard Sosi crying. I awoke to
find a great serpent eating her. Her legs were
in his mouth and he was swallowing her alive.
I jumped up, which scared Akosua. When she
saw the serpent, she screamed. The Trokosi
awoke and were terrified. One Trokosi yelled,
"Dangbe has chosen Sosi to be his sacrifice."
Sosi lay stiff, like a beam of wood. She was
breathing fast and crying. I was scared, but I
clapped my hands at the serpent and yelled,

"No, Dangbe, no! Choose another sacrifice. Let this one go! Do not take Sosi!" But he would not listen. The girls were frightened, because I dared tell the god to leave Sosi alone. But, the god would not stop swallowing her. Some of the Trokosi fell down on the floor before him and began to worship him.

I could not bear to see Sosi be taken in death by the god; she was as my own child. I did not even think about what I was doing. I ran out of the chamber into the shrine and took the sacred machete of sacrifice from the temple. I went back into the chamber and raised it over my head; I demanded, "Dangbe, let her go, now!" But, he would not, so I brought down the machete upon him. I could not cut him. The Trokosi started screaming for me to stop, but I would not. I chopped at him and his tail thrashed at me. He could not do anything, because Sosi was in his mouth. I chopped at him and began to cut him. I swung at the serpent over and over again, until I cut him in half. He vomited Sosi out of his mouth and turned upon me. When he did, I yelled, "Akosua, get Sosi!" She pulled Sosi away from the serpent as I confronted him. The serpent jumped at me and I brought the machete down upon his head, splitting his skull in two. The serpent was dead, though his body thrashed around the temple. The Trokosi were crying and screaming, but Sosi was alive. I dropped the machete and knelt to take her into my arms; I held her.

Kuuku entered the chamber. He cried out, "What's happening here?" He looked and saw the dying serpent and the blood. The Trokosi were on the floor bowing to him crying, but no one would answer. He saw me covered with the serpent's blood, holding Sosi; he saw the machete lying on the floor in front of me. Kuuku became frightened, "I demand that you tell me what happened here!" Akosua sat next to me and said to him, "Afi has slain the god, Dangbe." He cried out, "What have you done?" I looked up at him and said, "I did what must be done to save Sosi." He shook his head at me, "Girl, you have killed the great serpent of Dangbe and have refused him of his sacrifice. Now you and Sosi must die!"

I gave Sosi to Akosua, picked up the machete and stood up before Kuuku, "No, we will not die. I killed this god by my own hand.

If any god dare to come take me, or Sosi, let him come before me now and I will kill him too, just like I did this god." He was very frightened. He said, "You speak like a crazy girl. You have been cursed by the gods and must die. You have brought a great curse upon us all." I said, "No, I am not crazy and I am not cursed. If any god has anything against me, let him deal with me alone. I, and only I, have done this. No curse will come upon you or any others here. If the gods are angry, let them come to me and I will answer them."

The room became silent. I looked around the room and saw the Trokosi, who were no longer crying, but were watching in astonishment. They looked up at me as though I were a god. For the first time, Kuuku was afraid; he was not afraid of a god, or even a man, but of a slave girl. I could see the fear of me in his eyes. He saw all the Trokosi looking at him, waiting for him to punish me, but he would not.

Kuuku said, "For what you have done, there must be sacrifice. Surely the gods will punish us all for your sin." At that moment, I saw that the fear of man was more dangerous than the wrath of gods. I remembered how my sister was killed and how she stood up to Kuuku and would not bow to him; I would not make the same mistake. His pride would cause my destruction; not my sin. I knelt before him and said, "No, Mawuga Kuuku. If the gods know that a slave of the great Mawuga can destroy even a god, will they not fear the master of that slave even more? What I have done will bring you greater glory. How great is the god whose slaves are as the gods? I serve you and you alone." I lifted up my hands, bowed my head, and gave him the sacred machete.

He looked at me, considering what I said; he was pleased with my answer. He took the machete and said, "Very well, Afi. If it is as you say, I will become greater than all the gods and you will be my god servant. But, if the gods have wrath for the death of the great serpent, it is upon you only. I am clean. To honor his death, tomorrow we will make sacrifices to Dangbe, for the sins of all the Trokosi. As for you, I will let the gods decide your fate." Then he turned and left.

I sat down to hold Sosi. Akosua bowed before me and said, "It is true. You fulfill the prophecy of your mother. You destroy the gods." When the other Trokosi heard what was being said, they started to bow too. I said to them all, "Stop it! Do not bow before me. I am not a god. Akosua, you know better. You must never bow before me. Do you understand me?" She looked up and said, "Yes, Afi, I do, but you must listen to me. You are not a slave girl anymore. The gods fear you now; you butchered the god Dangbe with your own hand. Did you see the great Kuuku? He trembled before you. I no longer call you Afi Nunana, for you are now Mawu Latsola," which means the butcher of the gods.

TROKOSI

Chapter 8

The Stone on the Stool

After I killed the great serpent, my life was never the same again. The Trokosi began to treat me as a god. It was strange; they feared me. I did not like it at all. Kuuku did not treat me as a slave girl anymore. He stopped calling upon me to lay with him. I was glad that he did.

At school, the children even kept away from me; Nufiala noticed how I was being treated. After school, he asked me to stay and meet with him. He said, "Afi, I have been hearing rumors about you. Have you become the *stone on the stool*?" I looked at him confused and said, "The stone on the stool?" Then I realized what he meant. I repeated, "The stone on the stool! That is what you were trying to teach me. I now understand." He said, "Do you? Well, have you also learned the lesson of the gods?" I responded, "Yes, I think so." He said, "Tell me, what did you learn?" I responded, "I stood before the serpent god Dangbe and I remembered that just as the stone is not the eye of Dangbe, the serpent was not a god and I killed him with a machete. I also stood before the great god Kuuku and I wondered if he is not a god, but a man. The god Kuuku judged that I must be put to death and I refused to die, before all the Trokosi. I saw that he was afraid of me and he did not kill me. It was then that I learned the lesson of the gods. But, Nufiala, I must ask you a question." He said, "What is it?" I asked, "Do you believe in the gods?" He looked at me and smiled, "Afi, that is a dangerous question in this village. Do you wish to have me killed?" I said, "No, please tell me. I must know the truth. I will not tell anyone. What do you believe?"

Nufiala looked at me, considering what he should say. No one was around us. He leaned over and spoke quietly to me, "Afi, I am a guardian of the truth." I said, "What is that?" He responded, "I will be glad to explain it to you, but it will take time for you to understand. You must first complete your next lesson." I said, "What is that?" He said, "You must test the gods." I was afraid and replied, "Test the gods?" He said, "Yes, Afi. You have already learned the truth, the lesson of the gods, but you still have doubt that you must overcome." I said, "How can I do that? How can I test the gods?"

Nufiala smiled and said, "Afi, let me explain. You may not believe this, but I was once much like you. I once believed in the great eastern moon god. I served this god in a temple, much like you do now. I, too, had doubts in the god I was slave to and I escaped to travel the world, so that I may learn the truth. In my search for truth, I found a book. This book was written by a man from the west, who, like us, once served a god. As I read the book, I realized that there was not just one god, or several gods, but over thirty-three million gods and the whole world believed in all these millions of gods, even though I had never heard of any of them. Then, I read what he wrote and it opened my eyes to the truth. The man who wrote it said that it is natural for men to desire to test what they believe. He said, *'Humans must not fear testing what they believe. Every religion and every god must be tested and tried. Any god or religion that cannot be tested and proved is not worth following.'* He wrote that we must not be afraid of testing the gods. After I read it, I decided that is what I must do. I tested my god and I learned the truth. Now, Afi, it is your turn. You must test the gods and learn the lesson that I learned. Only then will you know the truth for yourself."

I asked, "Nufiala, what did you learn? Please tell me." He said, "I cannot. You must discover a way to test the gods and then you will understand." I replied, "Okay, but will you teach me more?" He said, "Yes, Afi, I will teach you a little, but I cannot teach you everything. It is more than you are ready to understand right now. First, complete this test and I will share it with you as you are ready. You are dismissed." Then, I left to discover how to test the gods.

Chapter 9

The Bleeding of Akosua

Often, I had been called to Kuuku to receive his seed, though I never bore him children as other Trokosi did. I was happy that I could not. Since the slaying of the serpent, Kuuku no longer called upon me, but the time had come for Akosua to be called. Akosua was younger than me. When the next season passed, she had her first bleeding at the age of twelve; she had become a woman.

Akosua was not ready for her calling, but she was to obey; it was expected of all Trokosi. She came to me and said, "Afi, Kuuku is going to call me tonight; I cannot go to him. I am going to run away." I said, "No, Akosua, you cannot do that. The priests will find you and will kill you. You must go to him." She said, "I am afraid." I told her, "I, too, was afraid when I was first called, but I lived and you will too." She said, "What am I to do?" I replied, "Go to Kuuku and he will tell you. Lay there until he is done. Whatever you do, do not resist and you will be okay."

Akosua said, "Afi, I do not think I can. I hate him. I do not want his seed inside of me. I cannot do it. Let us leave together now and be the wind. Your mother said that you would be the wind; she told you that you would fight against the gods and her prophecy was true. Let us go now and fulfill her prophecy." I said, "No, it is not time. Kuuku will kill us. We have no place to go; we have no place to hide in the jungle. The animals will kill us; it is too dangerous. The village people will not help a Trokosi. Out of fear of the gods, they will turn us over to Kuuku and he will kill us. You must go to Kuuku."

Akosua said, "Does it hurt?" I told her, "I cannot lie; it does, but not so much that you will die. The pain will go away; after the first time, it will get better. You will be okay, Akosua, trust me. After a while, there will be no pain and you will feel nothing at all, just like me. Let him finish and then cleanse yourself with water afterward. Soon, it will be no different than any other work you do at the temple. It is a duty that all of us fulfill."

That night, the priests came to take Akosua to Kuuku. She washed her face and went quietly. As they did with me, the priests performed a ritual to prepare her for Kuuku. The drums played as they do when a new virgin goes unto Kuuku. Then it was quiet, for a moment.

The shrine temple is small. All that happens can be heard throughout the temple. I knew that they had begun and I could hear Akosua crying. Kuuku told her to be silent, but she would not. She cried even more. She cried that he was hurting her. He did not stop; he yelled at her to be silent. Then, Akosua became as a crazy person. She screamed for him to get off of her and she fought him. She yelled at him, "Get off of me. I hate you! I hate you!" I became afraid for her. I heard him hit her many times as she screamed and cried. He yelled at her, "You dare refuse the seed of a god?" He hit her again and yelled, "You are condemned of the gods and will be punished forever!" He called for the priests to come in.

All the Trokosi listened in fear. He told the priests to hold her down. I did not know what he was doing, but I could hear her struggling to fight against them. He told her, "Since you refuse the seed from my staff of life, you will suffer the seed from my staff of death." After he spoke, I heard her soul scream out and I will never forget it. It was the sound that fills my ears to this day and breaks my heart. It was the scream of death, heard throughout the whole village. I began shaking and crying for Akosua, because I knew he had done the worst to her and it was too late to stop him.

Kuuku cried out for all the Trokosi to come to him. We were afraid for our lives as we entered the sanctuary. Akosua lay on the ground naked, with a wooden staff in her womb, piercing up through her stomach. Blood came from her mouth and nose. Kuuku cried out, "This is what happens to any slave who refuses the seed of Mawuga Kuuku. Look upon her and never forget what you see. Akosua dies this night, because of her great sin. She dies because she rejects the gods. This is a lesson to each of you." Then he turned and left.

I ran to Akosua and lifted her head. I cried, "I am sorry, Akosua. Do not leave me, my sister. Do not go!" She was coughing up blood and could not speak. She had the look of death in her eyes and I knew she was leaving me. I held her in my arms; tears rolled down my face onto her cheek and mixed with her blood; I shook greatly. I cried out to the gods but they did not answer. I held Akosua as she was dying and I said, "It is time for you to go, my sister. You are now free of this evil place. No more will you be a slave of the gods. You are now the wind. Be the wind." As I said that, the wind left her body and she was free.

TROKOSI

Chapter 10

Zombi

My heart became heavy without Akosua. I thought of her every day and I will always miss her. When I went to school after that evil day, I felt I was becoming the Zombi, like I had seen the elder Trokosi do. Nufiala noticed my Zombi face and he called me to meet him after school. I did not want to talk to him, but I went to him as he asked.

"Afi," he said, "What has happened to give you a sad face? Tell me." I could not answer. Tears began to roll down my cheeks. He said, "Afi, did someone hurt you? What is the matter?" I looked down and wept, "Akosua is dead." He said, "Akosua?" I replied, "She was as my sister in the temple… and Kuuku killed her last night for not giving herself to him. She refused him and he thrust his staff into her so that she died. My heart hurts, Nufiala. What should I do?" He too became saddened. "Afi, I am sorry to hear that. That is very upsetting. I do not know. Let us talk again tomorrow. Go and rest for now."

The next day, after school, Nufiala asked me, "Afi, are you ready to meet today?" I shook my head no and left. This happened for many days until he stopped asking. Each night, I lay next to Sosi, holding her as she slept, but I could not sing to her any longer. Akosua was gone and the song had left my heart. I did not want to think anymore. I was ready to become the Zombi; that was the future of the Trokosi and I was ready to accept it. I could not bear to think about what would happen to Sosi after her first bleeding. I did not want to think of what would happen to any of the Trokosi. The temple looked differently to me after Akosua died. It was an evil place and the gods I served were no longer gods; they were devils. I grew to hate them even though my mother taught me never to hate. I was ready for the serpent of hate to come to me and choke my heart; I would kill him as I did Dangbe, but if not, I was ready to die.

The next day, after school, Nufiala called to me, "Afi, come here. I must speak with you." He was very serious. I did not want to meet, but I went to him. He said, "Afi, it is not good that you have become this way. You were my best student. You must not continue like this." I looked down and refused to speak. He said, "How is it that the slave girl who kills the god Dangbe with her own hand and is a god herself among all the village becomes the walking dead? Do you not see that you defeated the gods once and now you let them defeat you? You are not allowed to give up. I do not permit it. I gave you a lesson to complete and I expect you to do it, do you understand?" I looked up, confused.

He said, "You were supposed to test the gods, so that you would understand the truth and would become free of this pain and suffering. It is only then, when you test the gods, that your sisters will be set free from Kuuku. You have lost your path. Tell me, do you think Kuuku is a man or a god?" I said, "I don't know. He has the power of death, like a god." He responded, "Then you, too, must wield that same power and become equal to the gods. Is that not how you defeated Dangbe?" I looked at him and started to think again, "Yes, it is." He replied, "Then, you must rise up once more and finish this lesson."

Nufiala then said something that I did not expect. I had never told him of my mother's prophecy, but he said, "Afi... you must become... like the wind." My eyes opened wide as he spoke, "The wind is silent and no one can see it, but it is powerful and can destroy whole villages. No one knows where it comes from or where it goes. No one can chase it and capture it. It is free. Become like the wind." As he spoke those words, my life came back into me and I saw the spirit of my mother speaking through him. I said, "Yes, you are right, Nufiala. I will become the wind and I will test the gods." He smiled and said, "You are dismissed."

Chapter 11

Fire Spirit

My next lesson had begun; I was to test the gods and prove that Kuuku was either a god, or a man. This lesson was dangerous. I thought about what Nufiala said. When Nufiala taught, he did not always explain what his lessons meant. He expected us to think about the lessons and figure the answers out on our own, but he always gave clues. Late at night, I thought much about what he said.

Nufiala's words spoke to me over again as I lay down. I entered into a trance. In my vision, Nufiala whispered, "Tell me, do you think Kuuku is a man or a god? Tell me, tell me, tell me…" I said, "He has the power of *death*, like a god. He has the *power* of death." I repeated the words over and over again, "He has the *power of death*." He then repeated to me many times, "You must wield that *same* power. *Wield* that same power. *Wield* that *power*." He whirled around me like a fire spirit on the wind. I whispered, "What is that power? *What is that power?*" He stopped before my eyes and whispered back, "Wield death!" Then his spirit entered into my nostrils and I awoke from my trance. I sat up and said, "Wield death." I lay back down and thought, "How do I wield death?" That is what I must learn to do. If the gods use death as their weapon to test men, I too must use that same weapon to test the gods. I must learn the ways of death.

I set my ways to understand death. I did not like death, but I had to wield its power. Death had taken Akosua in a bad way through piercing by Kuuku's staff. I understood this way of death, but piercing a person by a staff was not a power that I could wield. I had killed the serpent Dangbe by the sacred machete. I understood how to kill that way, but I did not think I could kill a large man in such a way; I would if I must. Disease had taken my father. That was a great power of death that I did not understand. It was one that I knew I could not wield. I considered all the powers of death.

I asked many Trokosi how some of their parents and relatives had died. I learned many ways of death. One father was eaten by a large crocodile. Another was bitten by a monkey and became very ill, until he died. One Trokosi's sister was bitten by a spider and died. Many wild animals wield the power of death. I thought on how to take their power for my own, but these animals did not want to give their power to anyone else to wield. I had to seek other ways.

One Trokosi told me that her small brother had died because he ate poisonous berries from the jungle. The deadly berries are what Nufiala had taught us about in class. I remembered how he told us that many plants wield the power of death; this was Nufiala's clue. That is when I realized that I could wield that power against any man. I could learn the plants of the jungle and use them to wield the power of death. I did not yet know much about these death plants or where to find them. But, I did know of one who could help me: It was the boy who knew all the plants of the jungle. I must find him; he could teach me.

TROKOSI

Chapter 12

Kofi

At school, I tried to find a way to speak to Kofi. It was difficult, because he was afraid of me and would not come near me. Even when he had to take a path that was near me, he bowed his head and walked around me. I did not understand this strange boy, but I needed his help.

I tried to look at Kofi and smile at him throughout the day, but it made him more afraid. I did not understand why. In order to complete my lesson, I had to have his help. After school, I went up to Kofi as we were leaving and said, "Kofi, I want to talk to you," but he dropped his school books after he turned to see me. He did not even pick them up. He looked at me like I was a spirit and ran away. I did not understand him. Nufiala saw Kofi run away and said, "Afi, is there something you need?" I approached him and said, "Yes, Nufiala." He replied, "Why did you scare Kofi again?" I said, "I don't know. He is a strange boy to me."

Nufiala laughed, which was unusual, because he never laughed. He said, "I think that it is you, who are strange to Kofi." I had not thought of that. It was true that I was the only Trokosi in school and the only priestess to ever attend, so he must have thought I was strange. I said, "I only wanted to talk to Kofi to ask for his help. I need to learn about the plants of the jungle and Kofi knows them better than anyone else, but he is so afraid of me that he won't even look at me." Nufiala said, "I see. Would this be for your lesson?" I nodded, "Yes." He said, "Let me speak with Kofi tomorrow and I will see what I can do."

The next day, Nufiala called Kofi to his desk after school. The children were dismissed and left, but I stayed sitting on the ground. Kofi did not notice that I was still there. Nufiala explained to Kofi that he wanted him to use his knowledge of jungle plants to teach some of the other children. He explained to him that he would be as his assistant teacher, helping students learn the types of jungle plants after school. Kofi became excited and said that he would like to do it very much. It made me happy.

Kofi said, "What would you like me to do?" Nufiala responded, "I would like you to begin by working with only one student after school, a little each day, until she has learned the plants that she needs to complete her studies." Kofi said, "Did you say, *she*?" Nufiala pointed toward me and said, "Yes, I would like you to begin working with… Afi."

Kofi turned around and saw me sitting on the ground and he became frightened. He repeated, "I… I… I…," but could not speak. He lost control of his bladder and could not stop. He looked around, as though he were trying to escape. Kofi stumbled over his own feet and he left. I was confused, again.

I approached Nufiala. He said, "Afi, I have *never* seen anyone have as much of an effect on a boy as you do." I said, "I know, but I just don't know why he is so afraid of me." He said, "Do the other boys treat you the same way?" I responded, "No. They are quiet around me, but they are not like Kofi." He said, "I think that Kofi could be afraid of you, but maybe there is another reason." I said, "I don't understand." He said, "Ah, that is another lesson that you must learn from Kofi,

on your own. For now, let me try to speak
with him one more time, tomorrow, and I will
let you know if he will teach you or not. But,
tomorrow, it would be wise if you did not stay
after class when I talk to him, okay?" I agreed
and he dismissed me.

Chapter 13

The Teacher's Assistant

The next day, Nufiala asked Kofi to stay after school. Kofi stood up and looked at me, trying to decide whether he should obey or not. I knew that he would not stay if I did, so I stood up and left. As I walked away, I could see him watching me to make sure that I had left.

The following day, after school, Nufiala asked both me and Kofi to stay. I did not think that Kofi would, as long as I was there, but he got up with a basket in his hands and stood there. He would not come near me. I approached Nufiala and he told me, "Kofi has agreed to teach you..." I became excited as he continued, "...but, only under certain conditions. You must stand facing away from each other at all times and I must stand between the two of you as he teaches." I did not understand, because it was a strange way to teach. I said, "How can he teach me if we do not face one another?" Nufiala said, "Kofi will pass the plants to me and I will hand them to you. He will explain what they are, so that you can hear him. This is the only way he will teach you. Is this agreeable?" I was confused, but said, "Yes, it is agreeable." He continued, "Very well, then, let us begin."

Kofi walked to the other side of Nufiala and turned his back on us. Nufiala gestured for me to do the same, so I did. Nufiala handed me a plant with large green leaves on it. In a loud voice, Kofi said, "This is the mangrove plant. It is common in the jungle and is useful for feeding livestock, making tools, and for curing illness." I whispered to Nufiala, "May I speak to Kofi?" He whispered back, "Yes, just do not look at him." I said, "Kofi, thank you. This is a very nice plant." There was a long silence; he did not answer. Nufiala said, "Kofi, you may continue."

Kofi passed another plant to me and explained what it was, too. After each plant, I spoke to Kofi directly to tell him thank you and I commented on how it looked, smelled, or felt. He still would not speak.

Our lessons went on like this after school for many days, until one day, when he passed a plant to me with large star-shaped flowers. It was beautiful and I said, "Oh, Kofi, this is the most beautiful one yet!" He responded, "Yes, it is my favorite, too." I said, "I can see why. Thank you so much for sharing it with me." He was silent for a moment and said, "You… are welcome… I hoped you would… like it."

The next day, after he passed a new plant to me, I said, "Kofi, I would so love to see these plants as they really are in the jungle. They are wonderful. Do you think you could ever take me to see them?" He hesitated, but only said, "Maybe…" I looked at Nufiala and he smiled at me.

Kofi began to open up to me. After several more lessons, I said, "Kofi, do you remember that Nufiala taught us about some plants that were deadly to eat and about others that could ward off their death attack, so that one could eat a deadly plant, but eat a good plant and live?" Kofi said, "Yes, I do know those plants, but they are very dangerous. I could not bring them to you here and teach you about them. You would have to go into the jungle to see the plants for yourself, so I could teach you." I said, "That would be wonderful. When could we go?" He did not know what to say. He looked at Nufiala to help him. Nufiala said, "Yes, I think that is a good idea. This is what you should do, Kofi, to be a good teacher's assistant. I think your lessons are going well. You do not need me anymore. Why don't you take Afi into the jungle to continue your lessons tomorrow?" Kofi nodded his head in agreement.

Chapter 14

Paradise

After school, Kofi and I met to begin the new jungle lessons, though we did not speak. I followed him into the jungle. We were careful to keep our distance so that no one would see us together. In the village, priestesses were not allowed to be seen with boys in public. It was dangerous.

After we were away from the village, I caught up with Kofi and said, "This is amazing. I have never been out here, so far from the village." Kofi looked like a different person in the jungle. He stopped, crouched down, looked up, and finally spoke to me, "This is my favorite place to be; this is where I belong. In the jungle, I am not afraid of anything. To me, the village is dangerous. Here, it is peaceful, beautiful; no one looks down at you; no one hurts you here. The wild animals are my friends; the plants feed me. This is my jungle."

I stopped and looked around me. It was beautiful, like in a dream. I looked up and saw

the many vines, trees, and flowers. The birds
sang and it was the closest thing to paradise
that I had ever seen. I said, "Kofi, you are
right. I don't want to go back." For the first
time, he smiled at me. He said, "Afi, you are
like this jungle." I said, "What do you mean?"
He explained, "When I was a small boy, my
father took me out here for the first time... and
I was frightened. I cried... because I was
afraid; I did not want to go. I had never seen
so many great and amazing things. I did not
want to be here. But, as my father brought me
out here to teach me the ways of the jungle
every day, I fell in love with her and realized
that this is where I belong. After I knew the
jungle, I was no longer afraid of her. She had
become a part of me; I had become a part of
her. This is how you are like the jungle."

At that moment, my heart began to beat fast
within me and I did not know why. I had
become afraid. I looked at Kofi and I trembled,
but why? I was not afraid of him, but I felt
different about him. I was dizzy. I felt that I
was becoming ill. I was overwhelmed by the
spirit of the jungle. What was happening to
me? I thought that the jungle must have had a

magical Vodun power over me, because this was not the Kofi that I knew in school. This was not the boy that emptied his bladder before me out of fear. Kofi had changed; he was different now, like a man, and I felt different too. He tried to teach me about the plants that day, but I could not listen. I was there in body, but my spirit was somewhere else, like the wind drifting as a jungle breeze among the trees; I was in paradise. What had come over me, the spirit of the jungle, I did not know. It was a new lesson that I had not been taught, but I would soon learn.

TROKOSI

Chapter 15

The Heart of the Jungle

Kofi and I escaped away to the jungle after school from that day on. I could not wait to be with him in the jungle every day, but I did not know why. I could not stop thinking about him and the way he looked at me. I knew that I was not a god, but when I was in Kofi's presence, he made me feel like one. I had never been with another man, besides Kuuku, and I had never felt this way about anyone. I had not touched Kofi and he had not touched me, but he made me feel better than Kuuku could ever make me feel and I had lain with Kuuku many times. Learning with Kofi had become a wonderful experience for me. He was a good assistant teacher.

As I had once asked, Kofi taught me about the death plants of the jungle. He brought me to one tall plant with white flowers; he said, "This is called the Onaye plant. It is one of the deadliest of the jungle. Its crushed seeds and hairs are used by hunters to coat the tips of their arrows for hunting. If the arrow grazes the animal, it will die because of the poison alone from this plant. It is very powerful." I asked, "If someone is poisoned by this plant, is there another plant that can save him from it?" Kofi said, "I do not know. I have not seen one. This plant is very deadly." I asked, "In school, Nufiala said that there was a plant that could poison and another that could stop the poison. Do you know what plants he spoke of?" Kofi said, "Yes, but it is not as strong as this one. I will look for those plants and I will try to teach you about them when I find them."

Kofi showed me another beautiful plant. He said, "This is a Moon Flower. The school book says it is called a Datura. The villagers call it the Zombi Cucumber." I said, "That is a strange name. Do Zombis eat it in the jungle?" He laughed and said, "No, it is because the Dzon'ku and priests use it for their Zombi rituals, to turn bad people into the Zombi. My father told me that a man he knew once ate of this plant and saw visions of the gods, but then he became naked and ran through the village like a crazy man for days. The man would laugh and throw his excrement at anyone who got close to him." I asked, "What happened to him?" He said, "He woke up from it and did not know where he was or why he was naked in the market. It is a magical Vodun plant."

In one lesson, Kofi met me and said, "I am going to take you to a special place today. It is where I go when I don't want anyone to find me; I have never shared this with anyone. It is wonderful, like the heart of the jungle." He took me deeper into the jungle through many trees. We came into an opening to see a beautiful waterfall, with many colorful flowers and plants. Yes, it was the heart of the jungle. I stood there, breathing it all in. It was the most beautiful and peaceful place I had ever seen. He said, "Come here," and I followed him.

Kofi brought me close to the waterfall; it was very high. In front of it was a beautiful flower, larger than any I had ever seen. I said, "This is the star-flower you showed me in school, but it is so big and beautiful." Kofi said, "Yes, it is the only one of its kind. I have never found one so great, but it lives here in the heart of the jungle. When I see it, it reminds me of you." I felt flush and said, "Why do you say that, Kofi?" He said,

"Because there is no other like it in the whole jungle; it is greater than all the other flowers; it is so beautiful. Sometimes I see it and think that it is so wonderful, because it grows in the heart on the jungle, but other times, I think that the heart of the jungle is so wonderful, because she grows in it."

I said, "Kofi, tell me. When we started lessons together, you would not even look at me. Why were you so afraid of me?" He looked at me and said, "Long ago, when I first saw you, even before you were a Trokosi, I could not stop thinking about how beautiful you were when I saw you in school. Every time I looked at you, my heart beat faster like the Vodun ceremonial drums. Sometimes I could not even breathe. I thought that one day you and I would be together, forever, even since we were small. I dreamed about you and me being together here in the jungle; I still do. I realized that I had fallen in love with you. When you became a Trokosi, I became frightened, because I knew that it could never be. You became the priestess of Kuuku, the powerful god. I could not come near you, because I knew that it would mean death for both of us. My heart was broken and afraid at the same time. Whenever I saw you, I could see the spirit of Kuuku standing over you, preparing to kill me. That is why I was afraid of you. But, I am no longer afraid. My dream has come true; I am with you now, here in the jungle. I am ready to die, if it means that I can spend one more day out here with you. Afi, I love you."

After Kofi said those words, we gazed into each other's eyes. I had never experienced a love trance with any other person, but that is what we were in, together. It was powerful Vodun magic. Our spirits stirred within us and we felt whole. It was the first time that I knew I was wanted and loved. He reached out his hands and we touched fingertips, for the first time. Kofi looked at me and said, "Afi, to me, you are the heart of the jungle; you are my heart. I have always wanted to tell you that, but I could not. Now, I am no longer afraid."

TROKOSI

Chapter 16

Master of the Jungle

The more lessons we had together, the longer our lessons became, until I returned to the temple, late one evening. Kuuku met me at the entrance and said, "Afi, why have you been so late from school?" I was not prepared to meet him. I said, "I have been staying after school for extra lessons, so that I may learn about plants." He said, "Is this the truth?" I responded, "Yes, Mawuga Kuuku. You may ask Nufiala and he will tell you. It is true." He said, "Very well, I will."

The next day, at school, I arrived to see Kuuku speaking with Nufiala early in the morning; Kuuku had brought another priest with him. Nufiala said, "Afi, good morning. I was just telling Mawu Kuuku about your after-school lessons." I was afraid, but I approached Nufiala, carefully. He continued, "Afi is my best student. She is diligent in her studies. She says nothing but great things about you to all the students. It is so obvious that she adores you. You must be so proud of her." Kuuku smiled, which I had never seen before, and said, "Yes, I am."

Nufiala said, "I asked Afi to participate in a program to learn about the plants of the jungle. Forgive me if I should have asked for your permission first." Kuuku responded, "I see. Very well. That is fine. I can tell that Afi is enjoying your lessons." Nufiala looked at me and said, "Afi, have you been learning from these lessons?" I was not prepared for what to say, but I responded, "Yes, I have. Thank you both so much for allowing me to learn more." I bowed down before Kuuku in front of the other students and loudly said, "I especially thank you, Mawuga Kuuku, for allowing me to learn more about your great creation. You are a great, kind, and generous god. There is no other more gracious than you." This pleased Kuuku very much, especially when he saw how the children looked at him in awe. He responded, "Very well then." He turned to leave and said, "Oh, yes, one more thing." He looked at us both and continued, "I have asked Dodji the priest to join Afi in her afterschool lessons from now on. He would like to learn about the plants too. Is this acceptable to you?" Nufiala said, "Yes, that is fine. He may join our class lessons after school today. I am sure my assistant will have some new plants to share with us." Kuuku said, "Very well then. Good day."

After Kuuku left, I was afraid for my life. I lifted my head to look at Nufiala and then I saw Kofi in the classroom, watching me. He looked at me like he did not recognize me. Nufiala helped me up and I whispered, "Thank you, Nufiala. You saved me from much punishment." He whispered back, "Afi, do not think that I don't understand. Remember, I was once a god slave like you are. I know what it is like to suffer faith. Afi, you know I will do whatever I can to protect you; I am a guardian of truth."

From that day on, we continued lessons in the classroom. No longer could we escape into the jungle. The priest watched everything I did. I could not even look Kofi in the eyes anymore and he would not look at me. He taught us about the plants only. I felt I was dying inside. I could not live like this. I was in love with him.

Every day, our lessons grew shorter and I returned to the temple with the priest, never saying a word to Kofi. One day, before school, I arrived early and waited for Kofi to come to school. I went to him and he said, "What are you doing? You cannot be seen talking with me." Kofi had become very serious. After seeing him act this way, I asked, "Kofi, do you not feel the heart of the jungle within you anymore?" He said, "I do, Afi. It makes me angry to see the great flower, the heart of the jungle in a cage, like a wild animal. It is not good." I said, "Kofi, the flower grows where it is planted. It does not have any control over where it is." He responded, "I know it is true. It hurts my heart to see the flower under the control of a terrible animal. It should be free." I looked at him and said, "Kofi, yes, instead, the flower should bloom under the watch of the master of the jungle who loves it. That master is you. That is why I came to you in the beginning, so that I may learn the power of the plants. With this power, I will kill the terrible animal that controls me. Then, I can be with the master of the jungle."

Kofi whispered, "Afi, I want this too, but you must not do anything foolish. We will both be killed." I said, "I would rather die, than be without you. I have to see you again." He responded, "Tonight, after everyone goes to sleep, can you safely get away from the temple?" I said, "Yes, I will do anything to be with you." When the moon is full, at its highest point, meet me at the heart of the jungle, but only if it is safe for you to do so. You must not be caught, do you understand?" I nodded, "Yes."

TROKOSI

Chapter 17

The Gods Have Spoken

After speaking with Kofi for the first time in many days, I became excited again. I was anxious all that day, but I could not wait to see him that night. I lay awake on my mat, waiting for all the Trokosi to fall asleep. Sosi was fast asleep next to me. I slowly sat up to see if everyone else was asleep. When I believed they were, I got up and quietly left the temple. No one saw me.

The jungle at night was a magical place. It was still beautiful, but also frightening. Many wild animals were out, which I had never seen during the day. The moon was full and it was not so dark that I could not find my way. After travelling deep into the jungle, I found its heart. And there within it, was my own heart, Kofi. He was lying next to the star-flower, in front of the waterfall. I could not help but to smile. I got on my hands and knees and quietly crawled up to him. He began to smile and said, "Afi, I know you are there. Do not think you can frighten me. I know every sound and smell of this jungle." I crawled next to him and looked down into his eyes. "So, master of the jungle, tell me, what are you doing?" He held up one hand and said, "Here, lay next to me and I will show you." I took his hand and lay down. We lay together under the night sky and I saw so many stars that it was impossible to count them all. I gasped, "It is beautiful." Kofi said, "Yes, it is, but its beauty is no comparison to yours."

At that moment, we saw a star shooting across the sky. I said, "Did you see that?" Kofi said, "Yes, my mother once told me that when a man and woman lie underneath the night sky and both of them see a star fall, it is because Mawu-Lisu throws the star down to the earth at the man and woman; it becomes the magical Vodun powder of blessing. She said that it is a sign that the gods had blessed them to become one. That is how my own mother and father knew that they were to become one." His words made me feel warm inside. I said, "Do you think that we will ever be free, to become one like that?" As soon as I asked the question, another star fell from the sky. We both gasped and Kofi said, "The gods have spoken."

I squeezed his hand tighter. I had never been happier than I was at that moment. We lay together watching the stars for a long time, talking about the things of life. I said, "Kofi, do you really believe in the gods?" He said, "How can you ask such a question? You live among the gods every day. Of course I believe in the gods." I said, "If you had lived among the gods like I do, you might see that they are not gods at all." He was alarmed and said, "How can you say that?" I responded, "Maybe we should not talk about it. I want to enjoy my time with you while I can; I must go back to the temple soon, before sunrise." He said, "Yes, but I must see you again tomorrow night." I smiled, "Yes, let us meet here again."

TROKOSI

Chapter 18

The Bone Straps

Kofi and I met under the stars every night in secret after the village went to sleep. This went on for many nights. I do not know how it happened, or who saw me or Kofi leave one night, but someone had seen us and they told Kuuku. I remember that day well. We were in class at school; Kuuku showed up with his priests; Kofi's father was with him. Nufiala approached Kuuku and asked him what he wanted. Kuuku said, "Bring Afi and Kofi to me now."

I stood up; Kofi stood up in front of me and said, "What do you want with us?" Kofi's father yelled at him, "Kofi, obey Kuuku Mawu-Lisu. Go with him, now!" We did not move. The priests came to get us. I began to go with the priests, but Kofi yelled, "No. Leave Afi alone!" Kofi was larger than the priests and he pushed two of them on the ground; this made Kuuku angry. I said, "Kofi, we must obey Mawuga Kuuku. We have done nothing wrong. It is okay." When I said that, Kofi went with them willingly. I followed in obedience.

Kuuku's priests took us to the temple. As he did, many villagers watched and began to follow us. Behind the temple was an open field with many barren trees; it was called the field of punishment. When Kuuku had taken us past the temple, I knew what was in store for us. I was afraid.

The priests tied our hands around the trunks of two trees and tore our clothes off, to expose our backsides. Kuuku picked up dust from the ground; he blew it at us and said, "The gods have seen what you have done and they have told me." I cried, "Mawuga Kuuku, we have done nothing wrong." He yelled at me, "Do you defy the gods? You have both been in the jungle together at night. What you have done is condemned by the gods." I cried again, "We have not lain together. Kofi has only taught me the plants of the jungle. No one can say we have done anything wrong; not even the gods. I am your Trokosi, only. I swear by the gods."

A crowd of villagers began to gather around to watch. Kuuku yelled, "Did anyone

see these two lie together in the jungle?" He
walked up to some of the Trokosi and looked
at them waiting for an answer. He said, "No
one?" He turned back toward us and said,
"The gods will decide if you tell the truth or
not." He looked directly at me and said,
"Trokosi, you have rebelled against the gods
before and have even defied the great god
Dangbe. Did you not think you would be
punished for your great sin? Again, you
challenge the gods! Now they challenge you.
For defiling me by being with this boy in the
jungle, I punish you both. If you live, then the
gods have given their answer, whether you are
innocent or not."

The priests played the drums. Kuuku had
begun the ritual of judgment. He cut off the
heads of two chickens and sprinkled the blood
over our heads. He threw two handfuls of
white Vodun powder at us and cried out to the
gods to decide our fate. While the priests
danced, one priest named Yao brought out the
sacred bone straps, which is a bone-handled
tool made with many long belts of animal skin
and bone pieces tied to the ends; it is used to
purify the wicked of bad spirits. I had seen the

straps used to punish evildoers many times. It was a horrible punishment to watch. Many times I saw men, women, and children die from the bone straps. The priests would use the straps to whip the evildoers until they looked dead. If they revived and lived the next day, they were judged to be innocent. If they did not survive, they were guilty.

Kofi did not say a word, but I saw the fear of death in his eyes. I looked at him and said, "Do not fear. The gods know we are innocent and we will live." I did not know if I believed those words, but I knew Kofi needed to hear them. I wanted to tell Kofi that I loved him, but I could not or it would mean instant death for us both. I had seen people tortured even greater by the priests if the priests thought they were guilty. I learned how punishment made people confess their guilt and the confession alone caused their death. The villagers believed that it was the judgment of the gods, but I knew it was the judgment of the priest holding the bone straps that caused death. If the priest thought a person was guilty, or if he did not like him, he would beat him harder and longer, even after he fell down.

The priest, Yao, who was to beat me, was a good man and I had prepared his food for him in the temple for many years. I knew that Yao did not want to beat me, but he did not have a choice. To make sure that he believed that I was innocent, so he would not beat us to death, I cried out, "Yao, the gods know we are innocent. I serve Mawuga Kuuku only!" Then he whipped me. I screamed as I felt the cutting of the straps across my back, but I cried out again, "We are innocent. I serve Mawuga Kuuku only!" Yao struck me again and I cried out the same words again, as long as I could. I felt the tearing of my back and muscles, even to the bones; the pain was so great that I could not stop shaking. The straps cut the back of my head, all the way down to the heels of my feet, until I fell to the ground, convulsing and bleeding. After many lashes, I passed out to go to the realm of death, but I did not die.

I do not know why the priest beat me first, but it is better that he did, so I did not have to watch my beloved Kofi die. If I had seen his punishment, as I know it happened, I would not have been able to bear it. Watching him would have been worse than suffering my many beatings. His punishment was greater than mine. If I had seen it, I would have done anything to save him and I might have even confessed my love to him before the priest, so that Kofi could hear those words from my lips one last time.

The next morning, I awoke. Nufiala was kneeling before me, washing my face with water; he brushed the ants and flies off of me. After I awoke, he called for a priest to come and cut the ropes from my hands. I was weak and could not lift myself up. I tried to move, so I could see Kofi, but I was too weak. Two of the priests came out to carry me into the temple. As they did, I could see Kofi lying on the ground, covered with blood and insects. Nufiala went over to see if he was alive, but I could not tell before they took me in. The priests gave me to the Trokosi to take care of me and to clean my wounds.

I was not allowed to leave the temple from that day forward. Kuuku said I was never to return to school again. I was in the Trokosi chamber for many weeks, recovering from my wounds. If it were not for the kindness of the Trokosi, I would have died, because I could not even feed myself for many days. I thought of Kofi always, but I dared not ask anyone about him. The priests watched me constantly. I did not know if he were alive or dead. My heart was broken and after I healed, I was becoming the Zombi again. I was alive, but my spirit was dead, just as I had feared Kofi was. I had defied the gods and they had punished me. I had dreamed of becoming the wind, but that dream was no more. I was only to be the servant of Mawuga Kuuku. Since I could not be with Kofi, I was forced to live out the rest of my days serving Kuuku as was expected of me.

TROKOSI

Chapter 19

Sosi's Secret

Another season passed. After I healed from my beatings, I spent my time with Sosi, when we were not working in the temple. Sosi was growing strong and wise. I decided to teach her what I had learned from Nufiala in school. Since I could no longer go to school, I wanted to share with her what I had learned, especially since I knew she would never be able to go. I still had some of my schoolbooks and I read to her as often as I could. Sometimes, as I taught her, I remembered Kofi and Nufiala and I missed them.

One evening, as Sosi lay next to me, she traced the scars on my arm with her finger. She asked, "Does it still hurt?" I looked at her and said, "The scars do not hurt, but they bring a greater pain, because they remind me of what I have lost." She said, "What did you lose? I replied, "I lost my heart the day I got these scars." Sosi was becoming a curious little girl and she asked a lot of questions. She continued asking, "How did you lose your heart? I see you; you are still alive." I looked at her and said, "Do you remember the day I was beaten?" She said "Yes, why were you and that boy beaten, Afi?" I answered, "It is because I fell in love with him and the Trokosi are not allowed to fall in love. That is why I was beaten." She continued, "How did that make you lose your heart?" I whispered, "Can you keep a secret?" She nodded, "Yes." I said, "That boy was my heart. When he died, my heart died too."

Sosi looked up at me confused and said, "How can your heart die with him, if he did not die?" I said, "What do you mean? He did die." She said, "No, he didn't. I saw him in the village at the fetish stand." My heart leapt within me and I became alive again. I said, "Sosi, are you sure?" She said, "Yes, I go there with Dodji the priest to take the fetishes every week and the boy works there with his father." I began to cry, "He's alive. He's alive." I embraced Sosi. She said, "Afi, I cannot breathe!" I pulled back and said, "You do not know how happy you have made me. I can't believe he is alive." She said, "So, is your heart alive again?" She made me smile and I said, "Yes, my heart is alive again."

The next week, Sosi came up to me in the Trokosi chamber and she whispered, "Afi, I have to tell you something. I saw your heart again today." I knelt down to her and replied, "You did? What happened?" She explained, "Dodji took me to the market and I saw the boy at the fetish stand. Dodji was talking to his father in the back and I whispered to the boy, 'I know your name.' He said, 'Do you? Then what is it?' I whispered, 'Your name is Kofi.' He said, 'That is right. How did you know?' Then I told him, 'I also know a secret. Do you want to know?' He said, 'Yes.' I said, 'Do you promise not to tell?' He said, 'Yes, I promise.' Then I whispered in his ear, 'Afi said you are her heart.'"

I asked Sosi, "What happened then?" She said, "He fell down. He's big and clumsy. He knocked over the monkey skulls." I was excited and said to her, "Then what happened?" Sosi responded, "He crawled up to me and whispered, 'Do you know Afi?' I said, 'Yes, she is like my sister.' He said, 'Can I tell you my secret too?' I said 'Yes.' He said,

'Do you promise not to tell anyone?' I said, 'I swear to the gods.' Then he told me his secret. Sosi stood there smiling.

I said, "Tell me, Sosi. What did he say?" She said, "I don't know if I should tell you. It is a secret." She smiled and said, "Okay, I will tell you, but you must promise to keep it a secret. Do you promise?" I said, "Afi, stop it. You had better tell me!" She said, "Okay, okay, I will tell you." She pulled me close to her and whispered in my ear, "Kofi said that you were his heart too."

Chapter 20

The God Game

Knowing that Kofi was still alive and that he loved me brought the wind back into my spirit. I no longer felt like the Zombi; I had a reason to live. I hated being a prisoner to the temple, but the dream of being with Kofi again made it possible to stay alive and serve Kuuku. After healing completely, I returned to my temple duties, though they were much greater than before, because I no longer could attend school. I spent much of my time preparing the meals for the priests and the Trokosi.

I worked to make Kuuku trust me again and I served him the best I could. I knew that the only way out would be for me to gain his complete trust once more. I began to ask him, "Mawuga Kuuku, did this meal please you?" I tried to get him to speak to me as much as possible. Often he would respond, "It was acceptable." If Kuuku ever told me that the food was good, I remembered so that I could try to make it even better the next time.

One day, after his meal, Kuuku said, "Afi, I got this book for you from the market today. It is a jungle recipe book." I could not believe it. Kuuku never gave the Trokosi anything. He said, "I know that you are trying to please me and I think this book will help you to prepare better meals." I bowed down before him and said, "Thank you, Mawuga Kuuku, you are so kind and gracious. I will use this recipe book to make you happy." He nodded and said, "Very well." Then I went back to the Trokosi chamber.

I was excited to read my new book. I could not understand why Kuuku had gotten it for me. He was not generous to anyone. I began to read it and I noticed that on each page some letters and words had been lightly underlined. It made no sense. Then, I read one page where some of the underlined words made sense when put together. They said, "that – you – can – not…" I turned back to the first page and read only the underlined words and letters together. It read, "afi – I – ho – pe – you – are – sa – fe – I – am – so – r – ry – that – you – can – not – be – free - now – do – not – give – up – ho – pe – I – will – get – you – more – re – ci –

pe – bo – ok – s – I – will – hel – p – you – ko –
fi – is – sa – fe – now – nu – fi – al – a"

It was a secret message from Nufiala.
Kuuku had lied to me about the recipe book.
Nufiala had given it to me. Nufiala knew that
the priests could not read well and he knew
that I prepared food for the temple. He had
realized that this was the only way he could
contact me. He had hidden another secret
message within the recipe book as well. It said,
*"To wield the fear of death is not enough. You
must wield the power of belief. When people
believe, then you have the power of death.
Remember the stone."* I was happy to receive his
messages. I felt that I was in school again and
Nufiala had found a way to continue our
lessons.

The next day, I was sure to praise Kuuku
for giving me the new recipe book. I worked
all day to make the best meal for him. He told
me, "It was very good." It was the first time. I
responded, "It is only because of your kindness
in giving me the recipe book that I can serve
you better. If only I had more of the recipe
books, I could please you even more."

I thought about Nufiala's secret message every night as I lay down to sleep. I tried to remember the lesson of the stone. The stone did have power over men, but it was not even alive. I had killed the serpent Dangbe. The stone did nothing. Yet, the villagers feared it could cause death, but why? I still did not understand the mystery. I was a person and the stone had more power over the village than I did. I remembered how the children spoke of the stone. It was the children who caused the villagers to be afraid. It was their belief that stirred the people up. I was not sure that I had the answer, but I thought I would become the stone and cause the children to have the same belief in me. It began with Sosi.

I told Sosi, "Would you like to play a game with me?" She said, "Yes." I responded, "Good. This is how we play the game. When you go into the village each week, I want you to tell all the children that you see, in secret, that Afi Nunana has become Mawu Latsola, the god butcher. Tell them that Afi killed the god Dangbe in the temple and that all the gods are afraid of Afi, because they punished her unjustly. But, you must not tell anyone that I told you to say this, or you lose the game. Can you do this?" She said, "Yes, Afi, that is a funny game. I will tell all the children." Then I said, "Now repeat to me exactly what you are to say." She did. Then I said, "If you see Kofi, I want you to tell him to play the same game with us and tell him it is a secret, okay?" She said, "Okay, Afi, I will, but I will beat Kofi at this game. You will see."

TROKOSI

Chapter 21

The New Recipe Book

I began studying my jungle plant books again. I remembered the different death plants that Kofi had taught me about in the jungle. I was preparing to complete my final lesson to test the gods. Sosi had played the god game in the village and she told me that she asked Kofi to play along as well. He agreed to play.

A couple of weeks later, Kuuku gave me two more books. He said, "Afi, since you have done so well with the last recipe book, I decided to give you another one. It pleases me that you have been able to prepare better food for us all. I also give you this blank book to write down new recipes that you discover as you prepare the meals."

I bowed down and told Kuuku, "Thank you, my master. You are so kind. I will not disappoint you." That evening, I read the new secret messages that Nufiala had left for me in the recipe book. He wrote, "Afi, I wrote to my friend from the west. You must write your story in the diary. He needs it to tell his people. They can help you. This is our only hope. With your story, we may set the Trokosi free." Nufiala gave me another message in the book. He wrote, "Remember, belief is a powerful force. I hear the children talking about you, Mawu Latsola. You are becoming the stone." As Nufiala requested, I began to write in the diary every day, when there were no priests watching. I quietly buried the diary underneath my sleeping mat after the Trokosi fell asleep.

One evening, after preparing the meal for Kuuku, he told me that I was getting better. I took the opportunity to ask him, "Mawuga Kuuku, I have better recipes that I think you would like, but I need to go into the jungle to get the ingredients. They are very special recipes. Would you allow me to go into the jungle with a priest and two Trokosi to pick the plants that I need for the recipes?" He looked at me and said, "I do not see why not, as long as you take Yao with you. You may take the elder Trokosi Nadege and Abide as well." I bowed down and responded, "Thank you so much, Mawuga Kuuku. I know you will be pleased with what I make next."

I had not been allowed to leave the temple for a long time and I found an opportunity to go back into the jungle. I was happy. This was my chance to get the plants I needed for the god test. I read in the recipe books that much of what made the food taste better also had to do with how it was prepared and how it looked. It used something called garnishes and spices, which I never knew about. The spices gave the food better flavor. The garnishes made people want to eat it. It was strange to me, but I learned how to prepare food in this manner.

I took Yao and the elder Trokosi with me into the jungle the next morning. We took several baskets and I picked leaves, fruits, berries, roots, and even flowers to be used as garnishes. Yao followed me and the elder Trokosi held the baskets when they were full. When I knew Yao was not paying attention, I picked from the death plants also. The elder Trokosi did not know anything about jungle plants. They watched me and even helped me pick some of them.

That evening, I made Kuuku and the priests a meal using the jungle spices and flower garnishes. They were happy and could not wait to eat it. The flowers made it look like the food of the gods. Kuuku seemed to like the meal, but he gave me an unusual look as he ate; he watched me as if he were bothered about something. He called Yao the priest over and whispered to him. Yao said, "No, she never left our sight. We did not go anywhere near the village and we saw no one." Kuuku called me come over to him and I obeyed.

Kuuku said, "Afi, I was in the village today. I am hearing strange things about you among the villagers." I said, "Master, may I ask what they are saying?" He said, "They are giving you a new name and calling you Mawu Latsola. Some of them are saying that you and Kofi were punished unjustly. They even say that the gods are afraid of you, because you killed Dangbe. Do you know why they are saying these things?" I responded, "They are calling me Mawu Latsola, the god butcher?" He looked concerned and said, "Yes, that is what they are saying." I said, "Mawuga Kuuku, it is true that I did kill the serpent Dangbe. It is true that I and Kofi were punished unjustly by the gods, though we were innocent. I cannot answer for why the villagers say what they do, but you know I have not left the temple or the presence of Yao the priest. I have not spoken to anyone in the village. I am only here to serve you." He was silent for a moment and said, "Very well, Afi. This was a good meal. You are getting better. But, I do not want you to go into the jungle for a while. Do you understand?" I nodded, "Yes, master." Then he dismissed me.

I did not know if I should be happy or afraid. The god game had played out well. As I had hoped, it was working, just as it did with the stone. The people had begun to believe strange and magical things about me. Nufiala was right. The power of belief was a strong force. Now I would use that force to wield the power of death and become free.

TROKOSI

Chapter 22

Testing the Gods

I lay down next to Sosi that evening and whispered, "Did you enjoy our game?" She whispered, "Yes, it was fun. Is it over? Did I win?" I told her, "Yes, you did. I am so proud of you." She said, "I beat Kofi?" I said, "Yes, you beat Kofi, but the game is not over. Would you like to keep playing?" She said, "Yes, if I can beat Kofi again." I responded, "Very well. Now here is the new game. I want you to tell all the children that you see in the village that Mawu Latsola is being held prisoner in the temple. If she is not freed, the gods will make Kuuku crazy and destroy the village with fire when the moon becomes full. Do you understand?" She said, "Yes, that is funny." I had her repeat it several times and I told her, "Remember, you cannot tell anyone that I told you to say this and do not forget to tell Kofi about our new game, okay?" Sosi agreed, and the new god game began.

I continued writing my story in the diary. The moon would become full in a week, so I had to prepare some of the death plants for what was to come. I decided to use the Moon Flower plant, what Kofi called the Zombi Cucumber. It would serve my purposes well. I dried the plant and crushed it up with other herbs so that I may use it in a recipe for Kuuku. I took one of the temple fetishes, a monkey skull, and I wrote a message on the inside of it. It read, "Go to the heart of the jungle at the first full moon." I placed it with the other fetishes that the priest Dodji would be taking with him to the market that week. I told Sosi, "When you see Kofi in the market this week, tell him I put a message in one of the monkey skulls for him. Do not let anyone else know." She agreed.

I only had a few days left before the test of the gods. I was growing anxious. At each meal, the priests were pleased at the food I had made for them, but Kuuku watched me as though he were becoming more afraid of me. The night before the full moon, Kuuku stared at the food and would not eat. He became angry and threw the food across the room. Then he yelled at me, "What are you trying to do to me? Afi, I know the gods are using you to make me crazy. Stop it, do you understand me? Stop it!" I fell to the floor before him and said, "I do nothing, but serve you, Mawuga Kuuku. Why do you doubt me?" He did not answer; he got up and left the temple. The priests all looked at me as though they were growing frightened too.

The day had come to test the gods. I prepared the best meal I could make for the priests. I lavished it with herbs, spices, and garnishes. I had made Kuuku's meal very special and had prepared it with the Moon Flower. That evening, I set a platter before him, bowed down, and said quietly, "To prove that I am your servant, I have prepared this special meal to comfort you and to let you know that you are Mawuga Kuuku." He was nervous, but he said, "The whole world has gone crazy, Afi, but I know that they are crazy, not me. I will eat this meal in peace tonight. I will show the world that no harm will come to me on this full moon. You are right. I am Mawuga Kuuku, the great and powerful god. Nothing can harm me."

The priests watched and listened to what Kuuku said and they whispered among themselves as he ate. He yelled at them to be silent. I stood back and waited. After a while, as the sun started to set, Kuuku's head began to droop. The Moon Flower was working. I walked over to the sacred machete and took it from the altar. Yao stood up and said, "Afi, what are you doing?" I demanded, "Do not move. The night of the full moon has begun. What the villagers say is true. I am Mawu Latsola, the butcher of the gods. I killed Dangbe in this temple with this machete. I have been punished unjustly and now I have my revenge." They looked at Kuuku and he saw me with the machete. He cried, "It is true! Afi will destroy us all! The butcher of the gods is among us!" He fell from his seat in front of us all and began to worship me. The priests were terrified and slowly started to bow on their knees before me. The Trokosi looked into the chamber and saw the priests bowing before me.

I shouted, "As I killed the god Dangbe, tonight I will kill each of you with my great Vodun powers." Kuuku looked up at me and screamed, "I see the gods standing behind Afi. They are here to punish us for beating her.

Please ask the gods to forgive us. Have mercy on us!" Kuuku was acting crazy because of the Moon Flower. He drooled and began rolling on the floor like a dog. He was muttering, "We're going to die. We're doomed. The death of the gods is upon us." This frightened all the priests and even the Trokosi fell down before me and bowed. It would have frightened me, too, if I did not know it was the Moon Flower making him crazy. It was then that I realized that the gods were not real. I had tested the gods and I knew I had the power over them to be set free.

I held up the machete with my hands and announced, "Kuuku, you are no longer to be called Mawuga, a great god. Now, you are Avuga, a great dog, because I have given you the mind of a dog." I looked at the priests and said, "Should I turn you into animals as well?" As they saw Kuuku on the floor drooling and rolling around, they were terrified. They cried out to me, "No, Mawu Latsola, have mercy on us. We will do whatever you say." I became angry and responded, "Have mercy?" I walked up to the priest Yao and tipped his chin up with the machete. I said to him, "Yao, do you want me to have mercy on you, just as you did on me with the bone straps?" He fell before me and cried, "Mawu Latsola, I did not know you were innocent. I was only doing what Kuuku told me to do. I had to obey or he would kill me. Forgive me, please."

I stood still for a moment and watched them all quiver before me. It was a strange experience, one I am sure Kuuku had enjoyed for many years, but I did not like it. It was wrong. I realized that he had used belief to wield death over all the people for many years. They were all victims like I had been. I said to them all, "It is true. I am Mawu Latsola, but I forgive you, only under one condition..." As I spoke, I heard a noise outside the temple. It was growing louder. I realized that it was the voices of the villagers, calling out to Kuuku. I stopped speaking to hear the sound grow louder. My time had come. I said, "Dodji, Yao, pick up Kuuku and drag him out in front of the temple before the people." I followed behind them.

After we entered the courtyard of the temple, the people saw Kuuku lying on the ground, rolling like an animal; he was pulling his hair and biting his tongue. When the people saw me step out of the temple, they started crying out, "It is true. Afi is the god butcher!" The whole village was afraid and cried out to me for mercy. Many fell down before me. They cried, "Please do not destroy us with fire." I held up the machete and yelled, "Ze dodoe," meaning, "Be silent!" They quieted down.

I spoke to the people, "Look upon your great god Kuuku. Do you see him? This is the man you worship. This is the man you sacrifice your children to. This is the man who steals your hopes, lives, and dreams from you. Does he look like a god to you now? I tell you, this is no god. This is an evil dog that I turned into an animal so that you may see the truth. I am Mawu Latsola. I now claim the power of your gods. I will have mercy on you all, but you must now obey me. Do you understand?" I saw Nufiala in the crowd watching me in a curious manner. He knew that I had learned my lesson now and I could tell that he wanted to see how I would use my new power.

The villagers yelled out, "Yes, Mawu Latsola, we will obey! We worship you." I quieted them down and said, "The gods have sent me here to set the people free. As of today, I free all the Trokosi. I turned to see them at the entrance of the temple and I said, "Children, you are no longer slaves of the gods. Go home to your families. I set you free." I looked out at the people and said, "I have used my great Vodun power to make Kuuku crazy like an animal to teach you all a lesson. Tonight, I will become the wind and I will fly away from this place, never to return. But, if I hear from the gods that Kuuku enslaves another child, I will fly back into your village as the mighty wind spirit and I will destroy you all by fire. Do you understand?" The people cried out that they would obey.

I pointed at Kuuku with the machete and said, "Do you see this great dog before you? Never forget what I tell you. In a few days, I will break the Vodun spell that I have cast upon him and he will not be crazy anymore. When that happens, he will try to rule over you once again and he will tell you he is a god, but remember what I tell you; he is not a god. If he tells you that he is, the priests must beat him with his own staff of death and then they must pierce his stomach with it until he is dead, so that he may taste the seed of his own death staff. Then you may choose another priest who is good to the people. If these priests do not obey all that I say, you must tie them to the shrine and burn the temple to the ground, because I will curse them all. If they remain among you, I will cast the Vodun spell over the village, so that you all become wild dogs. Do you understand?" They agreed.

"Now, you must do one last thing, or else I will destroy this village. You must put your children in school. Kuuku is no longer your master. You will now learn from a new master, the school teacher." I pointed to Nufiala and said, "This man holds the truth and he is now blessed by the gods to lead you into a new way of life. If I find that any of you hold back your children from school, I will become the wind and warn you. You will see me in the leaves of the trees. You will hear me brush the thatched roofs of your huts and I will fly into the windows of your homes to punish you for keeping the truth from your children. I protect the children and I will bless this village through them, if you obey my words."

The people were afraid, but I knew that
what I was doing would be best for them all. I
could not tell them that there were no gods;
they were not ready for that truth. I gave them
a gift, however. It was the gift of freedom from
Kuuku and his lies. I gave them a new
beginning, so that they may now learn the
truth as I did from Nufiala, who helped to set
me free.

I dismissed the people and went to Sosi.
She stood by her parents; I knelt down to
embrace her. I began to cry, because I knew I
might never see her again. I said, "Sosi, I love
you like a sister." She said, "Will I ever see
you again?" I responded, "When you hear the
wind, I will be there. I will never leave you.
But now, I must fly away. I can no longer stay
in this place and I can tell no one where I am
going. But I want you to promise one thing."
She said, "What is it?" I said, "I want you to
go to school every day and learn from Nufiala.
He will teach you many great things, just like
he taught to me, okay?" She agreed.

Then Sosi asked me, "Afi, is the game over
now?" I said, "Yes, it is." She asked, "Did I
win? Did I beat Kofi?" I said, "Yes, you beat

Kofi. You did a very good job. You are now free. That is your reward." She responded, "I will miss playing the games with you, Afi." Then I said, "Sosi, I will miss playing with you too. But, if the priests ever start to take the children as slaves again, or if they hurt the people, I want you to start a new game. Tell them that Mawu Latsola is coming back to punish them with great fire if they do not stop. Tell this to all the children like you did before. That will be our new game, but I hope you do not have to play it." She looked at me and said, "Okay, Afi," and she embraced me for a long time.

Before we departed, I told Sosi to tell Nufiala that I would complete the diary and have it sent to him when I was done. She agreed and I went into the temple one last time to retrieve the diary and my school books. The priests did not stand in my way; they were silent. They bowed their heads to me and then I left for the heart of the jungle to find my true love, Kofi.

TROKOSI

Chapter 23

Letter to Nufiala

The following letter, found inside Afi Nunana's diary, appeared on Nufiala's desk, approximately one month after she left her village.

Dear Nufiala,

This is the diary with my story written in it, as you requested. I wish I could have delivered it to you in person, as I have missed you greatly, but Kofi said it would not be wise for us to be seen in the village. That is why Kofi is bringing it to you at night.

I have not been to the village since the last moon, when I left it, and I do not plan to return, although I do miss you and Sosi. Kofi and I cannot be put at risk again. I will not allow it. I am happy now and free like the wind in the heart of the jungle. I am with Kofi, my true love. We survive off the plants of the jungle, far from the village. We need nothing else and we are no longer afraid. I thank you so much for your secret messages and lessons that helped me to become free. I am forever grateful to you.

I hope Kuuku and the priests are no longer causing the people to suffer. If they are, please ask Sosi to play her game with you. She will know what I mean. I hope she, as well as all the children, are in school now, learning the same lessons that you taught me. Please do not tell Sosi about this letter, because I do not want her to miss me and be sad. She must live her new life and forget about me. Take care of her. I expect Sosi to be your best student. I tried to teach her everything that you taught me. She is a wise and good student.

I only regret that I will no longer be able to sit in school with the children and learn from you. I think about your lessons often and the ones that I will never learn. There is still so much that I wish to discover. I had hoped to learn more from you. We never had that chance.

You secretly wrote that the man from the west could help free me, but I do not need his help now; I am free, like the wind. There are still other Trokosi in the surrounding villages who are not free, though. Please ask him and his people to save them, if they are able. If you think the diary may help to set all the Trokosi free, please share it with them. There are many others like me, who have suffered greatly. They need your lessons and your help.

Finally, I hope you are greatly blessed by whatever guides you in this world. I know that you are a good man and that many good things will happen for you. Thank you for all that you have done for me.

Your student,

Afi

TROKOSI

"30 million people across the globe are living in modern-day slavery."

Global Slavery Index, 2014

TROKOSI

TROKOSI

Marty D. Fish

Enjoy these other fine books by Great Hope Publishing:

Passion Formula – The New Customer Experience, by Marty D. Fish, CFE. *The Passion Formula reveals the means to achieving superior business success through excellent customer service. As "edutainment," the book is written in a futuristic, science-fiction style, utilizing solid business principles. It gives a fresh twist on how to grow any business by creating new, exciting, and passionate customer experiences.*

Snerfy Cat Meets Prancy Finch, by Mister Fish. *"Flick! Flick! Flick!" goes Snerfy Cat's tail, as he seeks a little birdie to fill his tummy so it "does not go Ba-Rump anymore." As fate has it, on this lucky day he finds just such a morsel, a sweet little finch named Prancy. In this fun and surprising little tale, Prancy gives Snerfy much more than he could have ever expected. Prancy does not fill Snerfy's tummy, "but his whole heart instead!" This is a bright, lovely, and positive picture story book, which all children will love and adore. It truly is a modern day classic among the world of hardback children's literature.*

The Transformation of Six, by Dr. J.D. Thorogood. *Experience the exciting, true life story of the artist known as Six, who shares his personal Sentrionic Transformation and adventures with the Centrix himself, Xion Armani.*

The Book of The Centrix: Xion Armani, by Xion Armani. *If it is a true story, as it claims to be, The Book of the Centrix is no doubt the greatest book ever written. The author is a man living between two worlds. "This writing is nothing other than my real encounter with a supra-human (alien) presence... I know this is all so hard to believe, but please hear my story. I hope you will take a moment so that I may share with you what I have seen, felt, and experienced. This book is my unbelievable experience into reality, a surreal reality."*

GREAT HOPE PUBLISHING™

Book cover:
    Photography - Clark Perkins
    Cover model – Brianna Williams
    Makeup, hair, and effects – LaDonna Stein

Paperback Standard Version
ISBN-10: 0985913754
ISBN-13: 978-0-9859137-5-5